Walter Morison

Through the Postern

Poems

Walter Morison

Through the Postern
Poems

ISBN/EAN: 9783337212735

Printed in Europe, USA, Canada, Australia, Japan

Cover: Foto ©Andreas Hilbeck / pixelio.de

More available books at **www.hansebooks.com**

THROUGH THE POSTERN.

PUBLISHED BY

JAMES MACLEHOSE AND SONS, GLASGOW,
Publishers to the University.

MACMILLAN AND CO., LONDON AND NEW YORK.

London, . . Simpkin, Marshall, Hamilton,
Kent, and Co., Limited.
Cambridge, . . Macmillan and Bowes.
Edinburgh, . . Douglas and Foulis.

MDCCCXCI.

THROUGH THE POSTERN

POEMS

BY

WALTER MORISON D.D

GLASGOW

JAMES MACLEHOSE & SONS

Publishers to the University

1891

My busy life has had a Postern-gate,

Through which, at turning of th' infrequent key

Of leisure, I have stolen to Poesy,

Where, the floor rained with rose-leaves, she has sate

In hidden arbour: on her simple state

Fair things attending, bright-eyed reverently.

Low at her feet stretched restful, then for me

The knocking world at my door might wait.

I mused in th' idlesse of the noon-tide air,

And if some fancy rose on jewelled wings,

I pricked it fluttering to the tablets there,

For the soul's cabinet of precious things.

Now draw I forth that to which haply clings

Mem'ry of Nature 'censed with fume of Prayer.

CONTENTS.

	PAGE
𝔓roem,	v
𝔄 Common 𝔏ife : *REMINISCENCES AND REFLEC-* *TIONS*, . .	I
𝔖onnets—	
OUR UNKNOWN POETS, .	55
MY BUSINESS FRIEND, .	56
THE YELLOW-STEMMED PINE,	57
THE PAST, ...	58
A "NEW THING,"	59
THE NAMELESS LOCH,	60
A SPRING FANCY,	61
THE SNOW-PATCH, . .	62
INFLUENCE OF EARLY MEMORIES,	63
THE RETURN, ...	64
TO DR. W. B. ROBERTSON OF IRVINE,	65
TO THE LATE PROFESSOR GRAHAM,	66

Sonnets—Continued. PAGE

" *WHITE LONDON*," 67

COUNTRY AND TOWN, . 68

THE FOREST-BLUE, . . 69

AFTER A STORM: MORNING, ... 70

BUT A SANDHILL, . . 71

THE IDEAL DAY, 72

A SCENE IN MIDSUMMER, . . 73

THE MYSTERY OF THE SUFFERING CHILD, 74

EVENING WORSHIP, 76

"*WHO DID SIN?*" . 77

OLD WELL NEAR GRAVESEND, 78

AT NETHY BRIDGE, INVERNESS-SHIRE, 79

CAIRNGORM, . . 80

ON KERRERA, . . 81

BEN CRUACHAN, ... 82

AT OBAN, . . . 83

AT BRIXHAM, TORBAY, . . 84

ON INQUIRING THE WAY AT AN OLD FORGE,
DEVON, . 85

A REMOTE WATERFALL, 86

AT THE CASTLE OF THE WARTBURG, . 87

WAIT ! 88

AT CHALFONT ST. GILES, BUCKINGHAMSHIRE, 90

CONTENTS.

Sonnets—*Continued.*   **PAGE**

TO A COMET, ...   91

ON INCHINNAN BRIDGE,   92

AT HURSTMONCEUX CASTLE,   93

PRIMROSE DAY: A PROTEST, .   94

AT RUNNYMEDE, . .   95

ON A FORMER BUSINESS COAT OF ARMS, .   96

AT GIRVAN, ...   97

THE HANDEL FESTIVAL, 1885, .   98

AT THE WATERSMEET, LYNMOUTH,   100

ON AN EARNEST FACE AT A GOSPEL MEETING,   102

IN WESTMINSTER ABBEY, MARCH, 1885,   103

"BLIND,"   104

LUX E TENEBRIS, .   105

IONA, ...   106

STAFFA, ...   107

STONEHENGE AND SALISBURY CATHEDRAL,   108

GLASGOW EXHIBITION, 1888, .   109

A SAINT, ...   110

AGE AND YOUTH, . .   111

AT BRANTWOOD, CONISTON,   112

ALL THINGS ARE OF THEE, . .   113

THE POET'S TEACHERS, .   114

𝕸𝖎𝖘𝖈𝖊𝖑𝖑𝖆𝖓𝖊𝖔𝖚𝖘 𝕻𝖔𝖊𝖒𝖘—

	PAGE
A SMILE, . .	117
MESSENGERS, . .	120
SIMPLE HAPPINESS, ...	123
IN A SUBURBAN STREET, . .	125
A WINTER MORNING, ...	127
A VANISHED SCENE ON THE CLYDE,	129
A NEW EARLY SUMMER, . .	131
SIMPLE WISDOM, ...	133
THE IGNORANT PEASANT, .	135
THIS GREAT SIGHT, . .	137
WHERE IS THY GOD? . .	139
ON AN OLD PORTRAIT,	144
𝕷'𝖊𝖓𝖛𝖔𝖎: *TO AILSA ROCK.*	147

A Common Life:

REMINISCENCES AND REFLECTIONS.

A Common Life.

WHAT have I done in the world? I have lived.

'What been? A man. 'Tis more to be a man

Than a great man: to think and feel and do,

Than think, feel, do a little better. More

The mass of the mountain range than the one peak

Uplifted on its shoulders and world-named.

Instead of great men, give us, God, man great:

The whole upheaved, humanity redeemed!

My life's been common: therefore do I write;

From myself telling what my fellows are.

He's most the poet who is most the man,

Knowing life's burden heaviest: carbon plain

A

Crushed into diamond is sole Shakespeare's mind.

Respect the passer-by upon the street;

A human heart is his: the dull outside

Of pebble is what you see, but, sorrow-cut,

'Twould glow or sparkle, giving back heaven's light.

Yet all are not mere splinters from one rock,

But individual, with powers distinct;

That has been given us we must offer up

In special service.   I do owe't to God

To be the man I am of all the crowd.

Each of us in the earth of his gross life

Holds some thin flakes of gold, it may be hid,

The earth the outermost, till trouble wash

In to the soul and bare the covered gleam.

Gather the particle or two; they'll add

Their little to the store of the world's wealth.

I too have had my thoughts, my soul has stirred

At fancy's touch; among the common grass

Of my plain life there has, half hidden, grown
A daisy or a violet here or there.

Gently a breeze rose this soft summer morn :
And now it swelled, and now it sank again ;
One moment it stole warmly from the south,
Another round yon bush curled from the west,
With it a leaf soft lighting like a bird.
Scent from the bean-field, freshness from the sea,
Wood-smoke from cottage, fitfully it bore.
"Such," said I to my soul, "will be the breath
That bears my verse: a variable wind,
Carrying some leaf, some scent, of memory."

I'm my own public; my own critic too.
Time was, perhaps, when I might faintly dream
My memory would leaf above my grave,
Green for a season; now I little reck

What others think of me : I know myself.

I sing much as the thrush trills to his mate,

Of love the song expressive, not of art;

Or, as not bird, but man with power to know

Of beauty, be there music in the notes,

I'm glad because of it the while I sing.

"Set down the score, then," says my heart to me,

"That you may sing it o'er some later day,

And one or two perhaps, of kindred soul,

May say, 'These are my thoughts, so have I felt';

Joining their voices pleased in symphony."

Seated upon a nurse's knee, a child

Some two years old, having put on my hand

A worsted mitten (still I seem to see't,

And feel it fleecy soft, and know again

The pride of being dressed so fine); that is

The simple shell I first find on the shore

Of memory.   It was a little world,

And I a citizen small, nay, king on throne.

The woolly glove was happiness to me ;

Fellow I was of kitten on the floor

Clawing with simple glee the worsted ball.

I understand its status and its peace,

And can bless lowly creatures in my heart ;

I for a while did share their little life

About the steps that led me up to man.

Next dimly the uplifting mists disclose

A tiny figure barefoot, held by the frock

Scarcely within the selvage of the surf,

At the sea side.   The wavelets as they came,

How large they seemed, threatening the ventured foot ;

Which quick withdraws at the cold-douching plash,

And then, full bold, bottoms the sand again,

And I wade out—how far to childish eye !

Ah, I have known since then this was my life
Pre-figured: how, held by another's hand,
I played within the marge of being's sea,
Knowing not its wide circle, or its storms
Heart-wrecking.   Since then I have been, unheld,
Swimming far out, and feeling at my mouth
Trouble's big billows salt, which near o'erwhelmed
Me, sinking in no looker's pitying sight;
With not a bell from my last breath, distinct
From the white waste of general woe, to tell
A corpse had downward sloped beneath time's shelves.

What I remember after this was weird
And gruesome: 'twas the first cholera time.
I mind me yet how from the evening dusk,
In field hard by my home, red fires glared out
Like monster's eyes, and smoke from smouldering
    heaps

Came in foul whirls. 'Twas burning of the beds

Of the plague's victims! How I, at my age,

Had knowledge of the meaning of the scene

Rembrandtesque, I cannot bring back to mind;

But all the years since then have had their leaves

Specked by the memory; awe entered me.

I was too young to think, but much I felt

Unquestioning. The smoke strewed on my soul

A soil of mystery, on which some seeds

Did fall, to germinate in after time.

From that year's haze stands up in sun-smit peak

Another memory, which fed with streams

My coming life.

Set upon shoulder strong

Of elder brother, in some vantage spot

Of public green, I saw a procession pass

In honour of the winning of Reform.

Trades followed trades, with their insignia

And blazoned banners, 'mid platoons of cheers.

My soul was stirred as then I did not know :

I only saw those waving flags, and heard

That tramp of men, those cries.   And still to-day

I see the crowds, I hear the far-off roar.

"Reform" was stamped on my unconscious soul,

And bides a flesh-mark ; and that tramp of feet

Has grown a prophecy of marching minds.

Speak to the young soul lofty principles !

Gild them upon your banners !   Utter loud

Great truths, incarnate them in noble deeds !

And God's elect of childhood will perceive

Unknowing; and at epochs new will bud

In effectual calling, fruit in works of faith,

The plant of heaven set in the true heart's soil !

I know not when it was ; I might be eight.

Upon a summer day I played alone

Near to my father's house.   And all at once,

As if a flame had broke through a heaped fire,

A brightness lit my soul, and to myself

I said, "I'm happy!" and I wished a friend,

Whose name I inly spoke, might chance to pass

And see me as I was; so full of peace!

Not since have I like feeling had so pure.

. Now, if the day be bright, I faithless say,

"'Twill darken soon!" if a fair child I see

Asleep in its cradle, straight its sunny face

Is craped with the shadow.—"Ah, this time next
    year

Its sleep may know no waking, the grave's worm

May creep across a cheek that does not feel!"

Knowing, I dread now; that hour long ago,

I felt and feared not: self-forgettingness

Rich self-possessing: then "eternal life"—

Being, without to-morrows or yesterdays—
Was tasted by me in prophetic draught.
Its sweetness bides within life's bitterness.

Later, one summer Sabbath eve, what year
I wot not.   All too full of life was I
To think of time.   Angels live not by weeks;
No sun to thin gold days shreds their one life.
Walk close with Christ, and till the journey's o'er,
You will not know 'tis evening : you will ask,
Did not our heart burn in us by the way?
The window to the north-west opened wide,
And I sat gazing.   The sky met my look :
We caught each other's eyes.   Liquid the blue,
And in it lay becalmed a far-spread fleet
Of many clouds : some stately, turreted,
Their solid sides against the clear relieved,
Some small, like little boats at anchor held.

Slowly they changed : great islands were outspread,

Fantastic creatures couching or rampant showed.

The sky was azure washed with green and gold—

God's easy fresco on heaven's western wall.

I looked intent, my mind sat at my eyes ;

Of poetry I knew not, scarce of awe ;

But both were in my soul in that fine hour ;

The sky a prophet's writing was to me—

That beauty is an attribute of God.

Long did I sit and gaze till slowly out

Died the gold glory.   Then the after-glow

Flashed up like diver, bringing pearls of stars.

The light is mystic, nor can ever fade.

I watched the rain one day, in midsummer.

The ground was dry and dust-white.   In the porch

Of a farm-house I stood.   First some broad drops

Starred the stained dust, then lost themselves updrank.

Some moments' pause, then warm gouts glistening fall
Like lighting gold-flies.   Fast and faster come
The impetuous pellets, lost in the floury ground,
Which blackens and smells fresh to my quick sense.
And now fine mist of moisture dusks the scene—
Trees, barn-roofs, hedges, cattle, veiled and dim.
Earth drinks its fill, and drinks my soul refreshed.

How hot the summer days of that young time !
The sun was not then old, nor did it touch
With bloodless hand.   Its ardours fierce I felt
Flung on my face on roadside patch of green,
When I could walk no farther on my way
Home from the village church one afternoon.
I could not even drag me to the shade,
But where I sank lay till my comrades passed
Out of my sight; when, pricked by the childish fear
Of being alone, I rose and followed them.

'Twas in the country, where, some happy times,

We went in summer to a homely farm.

Within its pleasant bounds there was a brook

I well remember, all its name, "The Burn."

Hidden it was by hazels; here and there

Cliffs showing, fetlocked deep with grass and ferns.

Up in the thick-wove shade there was a linn,

Black-red as blood: scarce would we venture near,

But in an opener space, where in gold stains

The sunshine lay, we'd seek with sudden hand

The infant trout, that on an eddied shoal

Of cinnamon sand, lay still as a sunk leaf.

A capture I made once, and feel to-day

The cold thing in my palm, and see its spots,

Crimson and small, dotting the pallid brown;

And I start yet, as it makes one leap more,

When I had thought that it had gaped its last.

In town,* what then the summer day but length
Of light for boyish games, or for late run
To Kelvin, rural still, for evening bathe?
Unmarked, though seen, the light among the leaves,
Sheen of the stream, the glory of the eve—
Miser with years, I count the treasure now—
All that we thought was—"Is there time to go?"
And "Will the stream be deep?" had there been
    rains ;
Or "Will it be too cold?" and "Who could swim
Across, and who could not?"   And, chief of all,
"Would certain dogs at gate which we must skirt,
Be loose or no?"   It was a foolish fear,
But real : sooner had we passed church-yard.
Ah, we were boys, and it was long ago !
Grown men, we have feared since, more foolishly.
And we have lost the wisdom of the boy—

                * Glasgow.

Of living in the present in God's world

As it lies all about us for a boon.

I thank thee, Teacher, for thy "Take no thought!"

Give me to use, not question about use,

Or structure, or the barren How or Why!

I chanced to see within a cabinet

One day a curio most beautiful—

A leaf from which the tissue had been purged,

Leaving a skeleton of frame-work fine,

Net exquisite of midrib and branched veins

That ran into each other, creamy-white.

But 'twas no living leaf! Its fragrance fresh,

Its fulness, softness, colouring, twittering, gone !

Would a bird know it? It is in its place

There in glass shade on shelf, its neighbours urns

With ashes of dead things in them. My God,

Give to me back, with age's measuring mind,

My boyhood's heart, that knowing I may be,

And that the substantial world I have learned

To analyze, I may possess complete—

Thy synthesis of sun and moon and stars,

And hill and vale, and shimmer of the sea,

And wafted perfumes, and the song of birds,

And the leaf living on the sap-filled bough!

What bliss it was in the vacation time

To leave the grim grey town for the seaside!

What talk before, what preparations made—

Purchase of fishing-lines, on square frame wound,

With "sinker" of bright lead, precious as gold;

Fitting of toy-boats with new masts or sails,

Or helm or keel, and many a pleasant care!

Then in the steamboat on the eventful morn

Of voyaging Columbus' soul was ours.

The sharp bell makes its last imperative call,

The gangway grates withdrawn, the rope's unlooped

From holding-post, its end dropped in the stream,

And straight inhauled by sturdy "hand," and wound

In cobra-circles on the deck bedript.

Now beat the paddles and the quay flies back :

We are away! And soon, beyond the smoke

And din of hammers in the shipyards, fields

In sunshine spread, with cattle grazing calm.

Then hills uprise, and the firth opens out

From where Dumbarton Rock stands sentinel.

The flood grows green, with bells of yeasty white

At prow and paddles, seething with soft sound.

Now sea-birds circle slow behind the stern,

Or slope their wings for sudden downward swoop.

Wind-like their shriek : Ha! we are far away

From the close town, like the wild sea-gulls free.

We feel the wind's hand at our lifted hair.

　Higher the hills and wilder, and the firth,

Lake-like and wide, white glistens in the noon.

Past Cloch and rough heights of Lochlong, we leave

Far on right hand dim Cowal, and sail south ;

Arran o'er Cumbrae grand and shapely seen.

Loosed now from Largs, we hold expecting way

To the one love of our untravelled hearts,

Millport !—let it be named as dear one dead ;

For dead is most that blessed it : though embalmed !

Close to the island's coast-line do we keep :

There the red rocks, the dark-maned " lion " there,

Couched ever, looking up on the low hill.

Round Farland Point, stretched like protecting arm,

We're calm within the bay, as now my soul.

Winter too had its charms : for the young boy,

Sliding with glee, his face red like the sun's ;

Then for him, older grown, walking abroad,

With eye unfilmed by grossness or thick sense.

Rime over all the fields ! the green shown through ;

Shed brown leaves sugared ; each sharp lance of grass

Fine-crystalled ; where a foot of passer-by

Has left its print, lies a fresh stain of green ;

Here, where the rain had gathered, a spread pool

Is glazed with ice, the ground seen brown below :

White crust in thinner parts : and, as I slide

With one wise foot, sudden round air-bells shift ;

Or if the heel rest on the doubtful sheet

A moment, hark ! it cracks, starred like a pane.

Red with his struggle 'gainst the morning mists,

The sun is free, and clearing his flushed face,

Looks kingly round, and where his strong eye falls,

The usurper frost straight yields, and the freed grass

Weeps gratitude.   But here, still in the shade,

Those bits of broken straw are glued to the ground,

Each finer-feathered than young dove's white breast ;

And this worn foot-spar of old wooden stile

Is silver, fairy princess might step on.

I saw it all; think not youth's eyes range wide
Unnoticing: I saw, and now perceive.

To-day a west wind smote my cheek, and fresh
Smelled the March ground, which to my printing foot
Felt firmer after the long-soddening rains.
A simple thing; no need for coloured words.
And yet to me th' experience slight has been
Magician's wand to wave me back my youth.
Just such a cool touch on the cheek, and such
A sense of foot that pressed half-stiffened clay,
Have lived in me: a small amid great things
Preserved, as in Pompeii by crust
Of ashes some plain jar near human form.

   And more! rise deeper meanings from the things:
The touch is from cold fingers of the dead;
The foot-fall is upon the earth of graves;
Old spring-times are in this new March; to-day's

Daisies root in the mound of buried years.

The past returns on us; make holy then

The present; for from the far under-world,

At beckoning of some finger of event,

Will rise its ghost for witness on thy soul!

The scenes of nature were as yet to me

But sights, not signs: still was the picture all.

Though that was wonderful; it took my love,

Not given yet to woman or to God.

Some meanings too it had, while yet of grace

No sacrament; imagination 'gan to lift

Its tinctured wings in my warm youth's spring air.

Rainbow that sashed the breast of Ethiop cloud,

Snow-flakes thick whirling 'gainst the gloom, a joy

Were to me; or in frost-clear night new moon

Held up in lake of blue, as in the tale,*

. * " Morte d'Arthur."—*Tennyson.*

Excalibur, or with the old moon clasped
Like acorn in its cup; red clouds black-barred,
Fire within cresset glowing; or a bush
That burned with sunset and was not consumed;
Or arching wave foam-crested, motes of weed
Or tangle in its amber, whole a breath,
Then clashing in a crystal dust of spray—
Such influences stirred me, like a wind
Rippling my spirit, as they had erewhile
Raised great still waves in Wordsworth's spacious
      soul.

Not he, or Burns, or Thomson, Byron, Keats;
Or Cowper, Milton—my home's household gods—
Taught me to look at Nature; her own eye
Drew my heart from me in a fond first love.
But books grew dear to me, as if they were
Inscriptions on the trees cut by her, dropt

Love-missives : these with rapture I perused

When with my mistress' self I might not walk

'Neath the soft moon or in the pensive dusk

Of mid-day wood.   From   them   I   learned   to

    know

Her inner soul.   I had but loved her face

Before, or flushed or pale ; slave to her eyes,

Sun-bright or their long lashes hung with wet.

But now to my instructed spirit showed

The deep things of her hidden mind, the signs

Which all sights are to him who has the key—

How things are double one against another,

And this is the meaning of that.   There burst

From the dun bud, which had been close, a bloom

Of bright analogies.   A prophetess

Nature became to me, like Miriam :

Clashing her cymbals in the glorious storms,

Singing her sacred anthem in all sounds !

My youth was pure in me, the outer world
I loved for itself, I cast a simple eye
On all creation, glad, unquestioning.
The morning air was sweet, the north wind's touch,
Cold on the cheek, was strength, quick'ning the walk;
The mountains were a glory: standing black
Sharp silhouetted 'gainst the liquid eve,
Or with grey mist monk-hooded, or their sides
Dappled like deers' by shadows of the clouds,
Or dark-sashed by a wood of pines, long drawn
O'er breast and shoulder. And the impetuous streams,
That, to the pibroch of their motions wild,
Dashed to the lowlands, caught me in their joy
And bore my spirit with them. The roused sea
Grand in its roar—what time the hands of storm
Freed from its prison the ancient phonograph
Of God's voice when He said, " Let the earth be !"
And the earth was—a prophet of the great

And the sublime proved to me.   Ah, fresh mould

Of youth, untramped as yet by satyrs' feet,

Would thou didst still clothe soft my manhood's mind !

My thoughts to-day be as the useful worms,

Taking the past, absorbing, 'fining it,

And throwing it to life's surface in new soil !

I did not question, sceptical, but much

I mused.   "Nature, thou art nôt all ?" I asked,

And this her answer : "I am nothing, God

Is all in all.   I am a bubble blown

By His great breath, of iridescence fair ;

And such are all the shining worlds.   We float

In th' element of His will our little while ;

We minister, by beauty and order true,

To spiritual beings, who will 'dure

When we have melted back into God's palm.

I teach thee Him !"   I bent my young brow bared.

Early I learned Thee, God, and in Thee found

The key of nature, reason, and my heart.

Thy mystery did not confound me : what

But mystery could'st Thou be, since Thou art God,

Thy "excess of bright" making thick haze of gold !

Thee to deny were to deny myself

In my deep being, which asserts Thou art—

The stamp which shows the Die from which it
    came—

I need and have Thee, and do know Thee sure.

Nor in cold being only: Thou art Light;

And, what had doubtful fallen from Nature's lips,

Spoke clear by Him who came to us from Thee

To tell us all Thy heart, I also name—

I call Thee Love! I know Thee Father kind,

And great as kind, whose ways are not as ours,

Since higher, on dread plane of perfectness.

The letters of the word which names Thee Love—

Illuminated word, of colours rich—

Are each deep-shaded, yet they spell the word :

The shading black to the tear-cleanséd eye

Making it stand out clear, confessor bold.

From its small pulpit-crevice in the rock

The harebell leans and preaches to me God

Who cares for great and little, and expends

An Artist's love on everything He makes,

A Parent's care on all He brings to life.

I bless Him that I have been taught to know

His perfect being as the Pharos light

White on the night's dark billows! He is thought,

And love, and justice, power; on the one throne

Of Nature sitteth Character and Might.

To bless thee in thy need He bids conspire

All influences of the universe—

I plucked of the grapes of Pleiades last night

And was refreshed !—and did their virtue not

Suffice thee, there still slumbers in His arm
Unspent omnipotence, which would awake.

   Great God ! the lowly know Thee and draw near :
In Thee the sparrow, fearless, unashamed,
Has its pert being, pecks from Thine opened hand
While Thou lookst smiling ; and against Thy foot
The kitten rubs herself, purring her plea ;
Thou art not angry with the jackdaw, that
Upon Thy church's steeple he sits black,
And croaks his dissonance with the anthem grand
Which hearts of men heave high in offering
Up to Thy shrine ! Because Thou art most great
Thou none despisest, to Thee nothing's mean.
Opens Thy heart like violet's, and lo !
In the dark velvet's centre burneth calm
A star of gold : love upon mystery !

   My God, I bring the oblation of my joy
That I did know Thee early, and have learned

To be familiar with Thee, as Thy child.

My Elder Brother taught me, when He came

To tell us we had misconceived Thy heart.

Guilty, we knew Thee righteously displeased

And thought Thou didst not love us any more:

Mixing the true with false; but when Thy Son,

Heart of Thy heart, came down to bear the brunt

Of what our sin had brought us—be a Rock

Against the storm, within whose ample cave,

Strong-walled, we could while the blast beat be calm—

Wonder rose in us, clarifying quick

To adoration, and we loved Thy name

Righteous and merciful, our Father-God!

'Twas like Thee to create, Fulness of Life!

And like Thee to redeem, Fulness of Love!

Ah, Shepherd-heart, that from the ninety-and-nine

Turns to the one that wanders on the wild!

See how that mother hastes at her child's cry,

Whom she could leave alone while stringing flowers

And babbling to them in its simple joy;

And righteous God, who hast had children, Thine

Is the prime Parent-heart, that pitieth.

And Thou art holy and the Lord of all—

Wilt Thou have sin within Thy kingdom's gates?

Sin more than sorrow pitying, as worse woe,

And worse than woe, Thou'dst purge it from the soul!

Holy, Thou'dst holy make, loving, wouldst save;

In us the need, therefore in Thee the boon;

In us the ill-desert, the righteousness

With Thee, and the sweet grace, which blot with
        blood,

Warm from Thy heart, the sentence on our souls.

The cross is the wise method of Thy love

In man's redemption: lo the tree of life!

Where sap of pity and strong righteousness

Runs to the fruit of a salvation just.

I pluck and eat and my dead soul revives.

Behind the tree I saw a glory burn,

An orb white-dazzling; but the screening leaves

Broke up the terror, and my eye could look,

And lo ! there rose upon the blinding disc

A cloud of the smoke of sacrifice, and I

Could bear the awful glory unconsumed !

    So was it at the first in my new life ;

But now such sense of pardoning grace so long

Have I enjoyed, that almost I forget

I've been forgiven, or ever did not love !

    We live by illusions : one is creature love.

Where Eve is there is Eden; she a spell

Throws over all, which makes earth's rusty ball

A paradise, gold-glancing for a while.

Love is that light ne'er seen on sea or shore,

Since in the heart it dwells invisible,

Making the beauty which it thinks it sees.

Peculiar bliss ! thrill of a spirit chord

Before unfingered ! There's a joy from flowers,

A glory in far view from mountain top—

Where lower hills, and plains deep down, and lakes,

And silver links of stream do dreamlike show ;

By music the soul's moved to ecstasy ;

As light in cottage window in the dark

Is a mother's eye, and sweet the tender touch

Of a young sister's sympathetic hand—

But they're not love, these feelings of the soul !

Or even of kin to it ; it is itself,

With raptures and sweet sorrows all its own.

Ah, those dear days when, from the darksome street

Beheld, a shadow shifting on a blind

Touched the soft soul to blissfulness, and made

Your heart say to itself, " It is her form ! "

Or casual meeting on the road sent back

The blood upon its fountain, and one look
From eyes soft-lifted taught you Dante's heart
When sunshine came with Beatrice's face !

Alas ! the shadow of the neighbouring yew
Palls the bright grass and lies across the beds
Of pinks and roses red with the flush of life.
Over my morn, the dew still on its joys,
Came in cold cloud the mystery of death.
The mother from our home—her quiet ways
Familiar like the ticking of the clock
Upon the wall, which ever filled the house
With its most peaceful music—sudden passed :
No more to move amongst us ; hushed the sound
Domestic ; and the silence awed our steps.
'Tis now a mellow grief, a solemn joy ;
Time has embalmed the smile upon her face ;
But that first sight of the still, stiffened form,

C

The movelessness of the white lips, that ne'er

Would part to speak to us, the icy chill

From the thin fingers, which had touched us warm,

Thridding the tangle of our pleaséd hair—

I know them yet, and wonder at my peace!

    Are there not pleasant ghosts? One came to me—

Or was't a dream which all the griming years

Have not bedimmed? In her accustomed place

My mother sat, knitting with useful yarn

And smiling on us. I beamed back with joy,

I learned what simple bliss the soul can feel,

Ay, and what grief renewed is! I awoke

The vision gone, and round me the grey day.

    'Tis natural a little child should sleep,

And easy for it, though the sleep be death.

So do I comfort me among the years

Over the little one whom God first took.

I seem to see the "Good Night!" which the eyes,
Weary with weakness, looked me ere they closed,
And I wait for "Good Morning!" with calm hope.

Later, the foe came in a sterner shape.
A preacher I had been, vendor of words,
And much had spoke of death, comforting souls,
And thought not that I offered empty pods;
When God flung down a sudden lightning flash
Upon the page whereon the words were writ:—
"As one that is in bitterness for a first born!"
Deep was the meaning scored into my soul.
For the first-born was mine. Up from the book
The bolt leaped to my heart, smiting it soft
And powerless: scarce I uncover now
The spot which tells where the shaft passed unseen.
It was in winter, the year's foremost month,
Severe: snow over all the land lay white.

And this year brings it back, a decade gone.

'Tis white again ; nor is it strange that I

Should see another whiteness—of the shroud

And trappings of a young man's funeral.

There is a mound where the snow lies to-day—

I mark it o'er four hundred miles, and sigh.

But spring is on its way, and the sad boughs

Will laugh again in roses : what we left

In the wintry ground, was not a withered leaf,

Whirled to the clay to rot, but a quick seed

To germinate and send up a white flower.

That headstone is writ rough with other names !—

Of parents : whom I bless in gratitude ;

And of a child who, when three black-robed months

Had pacéd slow after our first-born's hearse,

Was also called to pass through the dark gates.

April had come, and flowers and the young lambs

Were out, and hope was in the soft'ning air ;

But still she faded, for the earlier frost

Had chilled the life-sap in its hidden roots.

At last a day came * which made England grave,

For a great man passed on it to his Judge ;

But little did I mark the large event—

The register by other record filled—

That was the day our loved one lost the light

From her large eyes.   They had been dimmed
        with tears

(Ah, father's child !) when told she could not
        live :

Most human tears, which did not wholly dry

From the drenched lashes—nor were unillumed

By ray from the far land ! Her father's child

In natural fear, her greater Father's more

In trust that took her weeping to His arms !

        * 19th April, 1881.

'Twas spring-time, and wise faith has asked me since—

In death did not there burst another flower?

The fire's my garden in this wintry time.

I glance without, and all lies white with snow,

Accented strong by sooty trunks of trees,

And walls, and gable from whose shoulder cold

The vesture white has slipped.   There's not a break

In all the dull grey sky that bending domes

The town.   So, from the dingy plot behind

On which my window looks, to the red fire,

Heaped in the grate, a bank of flowers, I turn.

There glows the peony, the marigold,

The tiger-lily; that quaint-branching flame's

A stag-horn fern, yellow from withering;

And here's the blue-peep of a speedwell small

From its dark bud.   And all toss as in wind.

There's life in you, ye children of the coal;

Ye stir yourselves to cheer me this dull day;

Ye speak to me with tongues, "Be glad in God!"

Ye preach me Providence—from dark the bright;

Ye prophesy of summer from the beams

Stored in the carbon: sleeping light and heat,

To wake as ministers in winter's need.

I am a child, and have a Father's care:

He sure, whate'er's uncertain; if our rest

Is like the halcyon's upon a wave,

Yet we can sleep; the sea is in His palm.

A child is free of all his father's house,

And into some of its great rooms I've peeped

In travel, seeing their rich garnishings.

'Twas from the bridge at Basle I saw the Rhine

For the first time. I from its centre gazed

In the large moonlight. Leaning o'er the side,

I looked at the heaped waters whirling past—

Movement continuous. Sweeping in circles on,

The Rhine to me is motion, onwardness.*

I call it Time, and think how awfully

It rushes yet, while many a moon has waned :

Of those who trod the bridge with me that night †

All changed : the old passed out from mortal crowds,

The middle-aged grown old, to anxious men

Turned the young boys who paused by me and gazed.

Yet are there others on the bridge to-day;

The Rhine is full, and full the stream of life.

And shall the river flow, and men who think

Fail as the waters that return no more?

The being I call mine, my conscious self,

A passing flux from a cold glacier—God !

I had been watching from the train, and long

---

* "The great characteristic of a river is onwardness."—*Horatius Bonar.*   † In 1866.

Full keenly the far sky had scanned in vain.

Settling to mood of unexpectingness,

I had half turned away my head, when lo!

Something my eye arrested, far off, faint.

What is that vision low of billowy white?

'Tis fleece of cloud wind-teased; or—can it be,

That long-swelled wave, the Bernese Oberland?

Nearer we draw, dreamlike yet firm it stands,

Nor like a cloud changes or thins away.

The snowy Alps! they touch me from afar,

Like Christ at distance healing, in quiet power.

It is not height impresses me; low-sunk,

They tell by their remoteness that they're great.

They stand a great white reredos in House

Of God, before whose lustre mild my soul

Is held in prayer. I'm at the gate of Heaven!

Another sight scarce less did move my soul,

Pleasing by awe, as the far Alps with peace.

From Rome to Naples we were journeying,

And ere we reached the southern city night

Buried the landscape, and there was no moon.

Dreary the way till one by chance looked out,

And " See !" exclaimed, pointing with flush of face

On to the sky in front, in which there burned

A yellow-red too high for earth-fed fire.

'Twas like an orange banner whose tall staff

Was hid by smoke, or a cloud-broken moon

Of frosty crimson. I had at the time

Forgotten it, and so Vesuvius,

Sudden revealed, by pressure of surprise

Printed itself in colours on my mind.

The mount invisible, I saw the blaze

Alone, and it lives single in my soul,

As if, God's awful face by cloud concealed,

The Israelite marked but His eye of fire !

At Rome I sought the piece of solemn ground
Where Shelley's heart was still, and Keats sank down
Grief-wearied.
               At a flat low stone of blue
With greenery framed, I meditative gaze.
I see no words, "John Keats," with reverence graved,
But "Here lies one," I read, "whose name was writ
In water." So the sad slab moans. Why, then,
First of the treasures buried in this field,
Has that beneath this flag been by me sought?
And why, when from a trance of thought I raise
A tear-filmed eye, do I beside me see
Others who the same pilgrimage have made,
Even through the Atlantic's roar? And how
So readily, from my few broken words
Italian, did the sexton know my quest?
Ah! as by ours to-day, so reverently
By many feet is sought the resting-place

Of the soul's son of Spenser. No, not " writ

In water" is thy name ! Tear-channelled deep

Rather in Anglo-Saxon hearts, a fit

Strong tablet, is it cut ! Sleep comforted.

    The Cæsars' Palace ! whether in you Paul stood,

He Emperor, before mean Nero's face ;

And, Tre Fontane ! whether you mark the spot

Where his grey head rolled at the swordsman's

    stroke ;—

'Tis donbtful all. But this I surely know :

He trod the Appian Way, and his eyes looked

Upon the Tiber, and did rest themselves

Upon that aqueduct's calm strength, and glean

Beauty and power from Alban, Sabine, hills,

And peace from the Campagna, a green sea.

I gaze on these as he did, and I feel

His company ; they are a linkéd chain

Through which a current runs from him to me :
I know the fellowship of saints to-day.

I take a book into my hand and read,
And as I turn the leaves a stranger tear
Visits my eyelids. If you saw the book,
You'd wonder at my mood, for 'tis not sad.
This is its simple power, that it was read
Nigh fifty years ago, when life was young;
And now 'tis what is writ between the lines,
Or in the margin, all unseen, that moves;
In every word association's power
Pulsates. My eye falls now upon a phrase
Of plainest sort, and it brings back to me
The silver laugh of one whose voice long since
Was choked by the grave's mould; and this recalls
A summer by the sea, when it was read,
As I was taking up in hope and fear

The armour of life's fight, which not unstained
Or dinted, I must now full soon put off.
Old books have books within them; on their page
Lies touch of after-glow from the set years.

And can it be that I am old now, I,
The little boy of yesterday? I see
Him plain, playing upon the way to school,
A roguish light in his brown eye while he
A snow-ball throws, then walks demurely on.
My father became old, 'twas natural
That his hair should turn white, his voice should age;
But an illusion's on you, little folks,
That ye should think *me* venerable grown!
The looking-glass is never true, ridiculous
That it should paint me with a grey-beard face!
If I by feelings count, I'm younger turned.
Yet are there some things that do seem to lie

Far back within the mists, as if they were

Of a state pre-existent! shadows walk

Or sit, thin figures of the long-since dead.

Ah, me! I know a tomb-stone lichened o'er

And air-gnawed, cut with letters out of date—

A little child looks wondering at its age—

And the worn words tell doubtfully the name

Of a coeval, one with large blue eyes

Full of the morning, and sun-glinted hair:

I hear her laugh yet which said life and joy.

Strange that a gravestone in the clay should crush

Such violet! Mystery of mysteries, God!

Up the long steep of life, with boulders rough,

And here and there deceitful with soft marsh,

Or edged by precipice sheer, or torn across

By furious torrent, I have slowly climbed

To near the summit. Nor have toiled alone:

A gladsome band we were of boys and girls

When we set forth from out a father's door

And, joined by playmates, sang on our morning

way;

Breathing the air of pines, pausing to look

At bird, or squirrel, or trout in the brown stream;

Resting on bank of thyme, then up and away,

Breasting the first heights with a run ! Ah me !

Where is the company ? Death-weary, some

Were left by the way; others, missing the path,

In the thick mists still wander. I now stand

Near where the cliff sheers on the farther side.

I try to pierce beyond, but glooms that surge

And curl about the rock's steep brows, and ope

And close again, ever deny my gaze.

I know there's farther land, but cannot see;

And I am sure I shall be safely borne

To the veiled region from this precipice,

Be it by swoop of angel 'neath the soul

Bearing it gently in its mystic way.

I shall not fear to light: whatever world

My foot shall touch, it will be one of God's;

And He's the same for ever, everywhere.

A little babe, unchoosing, I did find

Myself in this fit house of Earth, with place

For me in it, a warm and soft-lined nest.

My small weak hand was grasped by one full strong

And gentle, my blind whimpering mouth

Was guided to smooth fount of nourishment.

There was sweet air to breathe, and there were
  flowers

To clutch at by and bye.   And all was good.

I'm the same Father's child; nay, nearer Him

By zest of reconciliation, and new heart;

And when again I'm born in death, not less

Will a fit home await me: should I fear?

D

Birth was no woe, and, able to be born,

To die I shall be able. Though 'tis true

I now am conscious, and have power to dread.

But I can take that black piece from the board

By moving over it this ivory white—

That I do know what God is: He who gives

Both lives, the present and the future, nor

Doth make by change the second shame the first.

My coming to this world I did not know,

I found myself within it in a home;

And in the far years of eternity

May death not be forgotten? With a smile,

One of the dwellers in Life's land will ask

His fellow from this far-off ball of earth—

" Can you remember when it was or how

That we came hither? Faintly I recall

A time when I did seem to fear some hurt

Was threatening me, and yet I felt no blow.

It was a darksome dream I cannot bring
Back to my recollection now 'tis day!"

A voyager far o'er the sea of life,
I drop enclosed this missive in the deep :
Will some one find it and the message read?
Hail and farewell, my brother! 'mid the mists
I in my destined, variable, way,
Rising and falling on the ordered waves
Of circumstance, hold on to my sure port.

SONNETS.

SONNETS.

Our Unknown Poets.

How large a bird looks on a naked bough!
An easy eye-shot is that piping thrush,
This first of March. But when, with sudden rush,
The leaves come out, gazing as I do now,
Their veil of greenery will not allow
Glimpse of the singer upon tree or bush :
Frond-hid the fount from which the raptures gush—
Fit emblem of our crowded age, I trow.
Great does a Caedmon show in bare March clime
Of England's nationhood; while in these days
Of life full foliaged, this rich summer time,
The wide air vibrant with a thousand lays,
Unknown's the source of many a tuneful rhyme.
Hid in the wood, the minstrel has no praise.

My Business Friend.

A LARGE plain house fronting the dusty street
Close to the pavement : tread of passers-by
Heard the day through, with huckster's summoning cry,
School-boy's shrill shout, and clink of horse's feet—
All sights and sounds of work-day world here meet.
But hid behind, a garden quiet doth lie,
With shadeful alley, box-edged walks, and high
Fruit-jewelled walls, that guard fair flowers most sweet.
Such art thou, friend ! Facing life's public way,
A plain built man, full practical of mind,
I see thee 'mid the clamour of the day ;
Then at hushed eve within thy soul I find
A cultured pleasaunce rare, where quaint paths stray
'Mongst flowers and fruits of spiritual kind.

The Yellow-Stemmed Pine.

Of all the trees here in these Surrey woods,

Scotch Pine, I love you! Not that to the North,

Dear with the years, you bear me, or lure forth

My spirit from the city to your solitudes,

To preach me peace in my soul-troubled moods.

This is the pleasant spell my thoughts confess—

You take the sunshine in its goldenness,

And hold it while each neighbour darkly broods.

So let me, one of the world's forest crowd,

Receive the radiance with a sun-ward face,

And when the gleam withdraws and trunks grow grey,

May passers-by, plodding with heavy pace,

Find in my look a brightness on their way

Such as is stored in your stem's ruddy cloud!

The Past.

Two little boys who sport this blue June day
In the long village street! Ye bear me back
O'er hill and vale of years by winding track
To burnt-out summer days of my far home,
Where lives my heart, howe'er the foot may roam.
I look—'tis I with old companion there!
I feel again the breath of th' morning air,
Though o'er me 'gins to flap night's curtain grey.
Play on, young hearts, with ring of voices clear!
Play on, play on, unconscious while you may;
Soon will life's bugle call you to the fray,
And then full soon the pensive hour be here
When you will feel the starting of a tear,
As you look on and see young boys at play!

A "New Thing."

Is there, still Preacher asketh, anything
Whereof it may be said, See, this is new?—
The sun which lights to lustre the pale dew,
Winter's white face, or this late-coming spring?
As once in Shakespeare's ear, the thrushes sing;
As now in the pied mead, the king-cups grew
While the child Cowper saw; and west winds blew:
Our fathers felt life's joy and sorrowing.
Yet, are not all things new to the new eye?—
Day-dawn, smooth leaf unfolded, evening star?
Look! was e'er seen such glory of the sky?
Some angel entering left heaven's gate ajar!
Keen to young heart the joy of so rich eve;
And ah! to me this soul-stound, as I grieve.

The Nameless Loch.

THOU too art fair, although thou hast no fame.

Rich the reflections on thy surface shine—

I gaze at jewels in an opened mine—

Heaven's sapphire, green of down-dipt trees, furze-flame,

Fire under water. Even as his who came,

Radiant unwisting, from high Horeb's shrine,

Thy face beams back the lustrousness Divine,

While no awed crowd by silence speaks thy name

So thou, my brother, stranger all to praise,

Far in lone place abidest, there to show

God's glory in thee through pretenceless days;

Not to be known e'er seeking, but always

That man in thee of the great Lord may know:

" Altar of earth," incense to heaven to raise!

A Spring Fancy.

A TREE stood looking at its fallen leaves—
Rachel bereaved and bare, her children gone :
Pity her there, staring with eyes of stone !
Shivering heart-cold, all comfortless she grieves,
Nor in spring's resurrection-joy believes.
But, see, with swift white foot comes sunshine on,
And stays with solace warm her mother-moan ;
Round her chill limbs he consolation weaves.
Sad soul, have hope ! Stript by the robber wind,
New joys will leaf thy winter-naked boughs,
Young tendril loves thy happy arms will bind :
Fresh fruit of faithful summer's marriage vows.
Add not despair to worst bereavement's pain ;
Glad thou wilt stand in foliage full again !

The Snow-Patch.

ALL melted, save this last wreath in the shade
Of deep-browed bank, that shuts out the soft south,
And the warm breath of the sun's passionate mouth
Kissing to life again the earth, death-laid.
While fields show brown or shot with glancing green,
Here, like white hare, these twin tall trees between,
Couches the snow, hiding in shady lair
From the feared shafts of the heat-darting air.
Thus, in a heart to the whole world else kind,
Cold hate towards one, long lingering we find;
Or freezing fear not yet heaven-sunned away;
Or icy doubt unthawed from the hard mind.
Late lies some snow-drift on our life's spring day :
An edge of north cuts in its westered wind.

Influence of Early Memories.

WHY do I love thee, Scotland?—For thy dark
Mist-marled peaks, or thy round pastoral hills,
Asleep in the heat, lulled by the low-voiced rills?
For curlew's cry? or home-sound of the lark,
Mingled from far with sheep-dog's echoing bark?
For gleaming tide which the loch's spread palm fills,
Or brown-black burn from the mossed rock that spills,
Or pluméd pine watching on cliff-top stark?
Dear are they all to me, my native land!
But to furred Lapp as dear his constant snows,
To Arab his desert dancing in noon's blaze,
To South Sea Islander his surf-laced strand.
This is the charm, which ever the heart more knows—
I looked upon thee first with childhood's gaze!

The Return.

Up from the village by the road to th' mill

I saw him pass, as one who knew the way,

Yet doubtfully;—change had been since his day.

Long does he gaze at the old wheel, now still,

And idle stream lamenting down the hill.

Next, by an apple-tree, time-crusted grey,

He pensive stands, as who doth inly pray,

While thoughts, far-welled, his soul o'er-flowing fill.

Here was he born.   Bough of that tree had held

A casket hid—a nest he one day found

With sapphire eggs.   Salt were his boyish tears,

The treasure gone!   So has his bosom swelled

This eve, back in the loneliness of years,

To see the nest of Home torn on the ground!

To Dr. W. B. Robertson

OF IRVINE.

WEST CALDER Station. " Pit with smoking stalk !

The country's face grimed by hands work-a-day !

Midlothian, too, where Gladstone wageth fray

Political !" Thus, as alone I walk

Musing, I to myself for company talk.

Next well-farmed fields, with belts of sheltering wood,

Engage reflection to another mood ;

Poising itself o'er nature, as yon hawk

Over its quarry. Now before me swings

A rustic gate, and winding avenue long

I traverse, greeted by late robin's song,

Till rose-hung porch me to thy presence brings,

Thy pictures, casts, books, music rare among—

I hail thee, true divine, friend of all human things !

E

To the late Professor Graham.

Six short months since we spoke together, friend—
As flower in fallen earth the memory clings—
Earnestly asking of deep-hidden things:
Of life, of death—there is our road to end?
Or shall the soul the frowning cliff transcend,
From the broke chrysalis finding sudden wings?
Useless always were our imaginings,
And in some jest did the strained soul unbend.
Now thou, my brother, knowest that which lies
Behind the height.   What is it?   Thou too still!
Conspirator, to glad me with surprise
When I in turn can see beyond the hill!
Thou'lt meet me with a holy jest again,
That we could e'er have feared our hope was vain.

"White London."

FIX it in memory! soon will mélt away
The frost-work vision this morn meeting me.
The roofs deep-eaved with snow, and glisteringly
Fringe of clear icicles stretched in long array—
Harp-strings of silver on which north winds play.
As with sloe-blossom burdened bush and tree,
And whiteness, whiteness, far as eye can see!
Foul London looks a holy place to-day.
This New Jerusalem has come from Heaven;
Waking from sleep I found the God-spread scene.
And when, Great Father, boon by love's might given,
Will London show of purity the sheen,
Its snow into each blackest nook grace-driven?
Oh, from all leper-whiteness make us clean!

Country and Town.

My window looks out on a London street,

Yet what I view is not the brick-walled way,

With those who pace it through the uncoloured day.

Mine eye the sun's o'er-flushed Cairngorm doth greet,

Or blue Loch Morlich's opening at his feet;

Like flash of fish, I see the silver Spey

Gleam from the wood; I see great boulders grey;

And haze-soft line where plain and mountain meet.

Drinking by day the sharp-sweet Northern air,

Hushed by low voice of pines at night to rest,

Let me no longer know grim London's care,

No longer by its horrors be opprest!—

And cease the city's griefs with Christ to share?

Leave Him sin's head sunk on His lonely breast?

The Forest-Blue.

OH chiefest charm of the far view serene!

Fair are the trees, and that white brow of hill,

Glassed in the stream spread out so clear and still;

But thou soft blue held mystical between,

Like cottage smoke at evening 'mid the green,

Or mist of hyacinths which spring woods fill,

Taking me captive at thy beauty's will,

Bearest me to the dear days that have been.

Scenes of my youth, ye stand amid such blue!

I see you dim and tender in its haze.

Such magic mist, old friends, enshroudeth you!

But most, as in the sapphire depths I gaze,

I see, suffused the natural landscape through,

A PRESENCE pure that awes my soul to praise!

After a Storm: Morning.

THE sky looks bright, as if it had not sinned.

Yet what a hideous and guilty night

It was! The infuriate elements did fight.

Flashed lightning's twisted spear; the wounded wind

Yelled at the thunder; hissed the sea, and grinned

With white-frothed teeth of rocks, which bite

Did at the billows, that howled back in fright.

Then contrite wept the storm, and the clouds thinned.

May I, as does this morn, show sunny face,

And eyes unringed with red, life's passion past;

No moan recurring of yet unlaid blast;

Of cloud of sullenness or fear no trace

Dark trailing. Fair in the free light of grace

Let my soul smile as ne'er by sin o'ercast!

But a Sandhill.

'TIS only a low dune, wind-scooped and bare,

The bunching bent in struggling patches seen,

Blown yellow sand in barren breadths between.

Yes, that is all; and over it grey air,

In front grey sea.   Yet to me 'tis more fair,

This pensive hour, than fairest spot has been,

Bearing me to the years ere o'er life's green

The surly blasts of time swept sands of care.

On such a mound, in summers far away,

With you, my brothers and my sisters three,

I was a glad unconscious child at play;

And now, returning late this autumn day,

Your laugh I hear, your little forms I see,

In ray through th' evening cloud striking the grey.

The Ideal Day.

In June, in midsummer, it needs must be.

Cloudless concave of blue, aërial, clear;

Landscape seen not too distant nor too near;

A light west wind soft fanning fitfully;

The long grass lush; one round rose the rose-tree:

The fulness and the calm of the poised year,

Ere yet descendeth winterwards the sphere,

And a great peace of soul possessing me!

Thus learn I Heaven. Of its white-footed days

This has stepped down to earth with print of bliss;

And though the messenger no long while stays,

And I to-morrow may his presence miss,

Yet do I know of Heaven now always

That its gold year is linked of days like this.

A Scene in Midsummer.

It was so beautiful I felt afraid !
It met me unawares, like grave fair face
Turned sudden round.   From a high open space
I chanced to look.   Far ridge, with wood and glade,
And fields in foreground, panorama made
Blue-misted.   After me one checked his pace,
And stood eye-fixed as in enchanted place,
Then turning to me, "Gate of Heaven !" said.
Landscape of dreamland, distant soft and still !
Nature speaks not to-day, but looks, with calm
Great eyes, which hypnotise me to her will
Of rest.   Upon my soul there lies the balm
Of beauty and silence ; peace doth my spirit fill,
As if there just had ceased a holy psalm.

The Mystery of the Suffering Child.
ON A PICTURE OF AN OUTCAST.

I.

Oh, little one, forsaken and so lone,

Hiding thy unloved face—thy poor young heart

Learning despair untimely, thine no part

In childhood's coloured joys—thou question'st not

Why thou art here, or whence thy piteous lot;

Just knowing grief, thy world a ring of gloom,

Thy naked feet thrust from the unchosen womb

To touch the cold of this hard planet's stone!

My God, forgive me that I do not understand;

But, tear-blind, walk in faith of Thy great love

Which gave Thy Son to sorrow for our sake!

Help me, so feeble, to be as the hand

By which the orphan-souled Thou dost up take,

And lift to light, where we shall know, above!

II.

THEIR angels always do behold God's face:

And, hand to sword, AVENGER, by lit eye,

Asks that, as lightning flash, he fierce may fly

And smite the ostrich-hearts which on the stone

Have left this little one, despairing, lone,

Praying in sobs to Heaven. Then pitying DEATH,

Angel of soft black wing, low-whispering saith,

" Let my arms comfort her with their embrace!"

But thus the Father unto them replies—

" Her angel walks the earth with seeking eyes,

MERCY his name, ever in steps of Christ

Treading bare-foot, with sorrow to keep tryst!"

As spring the deep-sunk roots by its warm breath,

Love finds the wretched out in hidden place.

Evening Worship.

ON A PICTURE OF A SEAMSTRESS.

Dim yellow candle, fouled, for that no time

To trim thee from her stern task could she spare;

Burnt low in marking the slow hours of care—

Thou shinest on an altar! And sublime

As star-browed seraph's at creation's prime,

The thin submissive face sad bending there

Over the work spread on the aching knee!

Altar-cloth makes thy needle, holily;

Or ephod for thy Samuel, by thy chair

Asleep in the curtaining dark; or mantle rare

To cover a husband's and a father's sin;

Or, ah! prove it a shroud to wind thee in,

'Twill turn into a heavenly garment fair,

Whose threads of light Christ's nail-pierced hands

did spin!

"𝕎ho 𝔻id 𝕊in?"

ON A PICTURE OF A SLEEPING BEGGAR-BOY.

Oh! weary, weary face, which not e'en sleep—

No sleep less deep than death's—from pain can
smooth!

Poor child! no mother's tones thy sorrows soothe!

Grief has itself run dry : thou dost not weep!

Swept in this corner here, a piteous heap,

As if no jewel lay the dust within!

My righteous Master, tell me, "Who did sin,"

That, a mere child, to battle thus with life,

Forth he's been thrust, to sink in th' unfair strife?

Not the poor boy, heir of entailéd woe;

Or his dead mother, robbed of the pride of wife.

Perchance the hard sinner passes, and a blow

From the child's hand strikes to his coward heart!

Or is it thou, Christ's Church, who the transgressor art?

Old Well near Gravesend.

WHERE pilgrims drank, to Canterbury bound—

Nun, friar, franklin, miller, all the old

Troop of "religious" by our Chaucer told—

I drink to-day. Refreshed, their tongues they found,

And passed the way-beguiling story round;

Flung feathered jest; spake deed of soldier bold

Or courtier's guile, never on parchment scrolled.

Echoing from Time's grey wall their laughters sound.

Such Well, great Geoffrey, are thy Tales to me;

This noon I quaff where pilgrims of life's road,

Dim centuries since stretched themselves restfully,

Unstrapped a little while their dusty load.

I taste, as they, the waters fresh and free

From human fount on the way to shrine of God.

At Nethy Bridge, Inverness-shire

ANYTHING written ? asks my friend of me

In letter lighting here in far Strathspey :

(He knew the sonnet as my somewhiles play.)

And this my answer fortunate may be :—

Not one poor line ; unto me spirit free,

Careless of fruitage, each gold flower-day

Opening and closing in its calyx grey ;

I write not, think not, look not, only see.

Yet is there that's been written : on my soul

Black mountains forest-furred, wild loch's eye-gleam,

Red Sea of heather covering flat and knoll,

Cot, farmhouse, corn-field silver-edged with stream,

Are pencilled fadelessly by heaven's beam.

Memory, well-pleased, doth the writ page up-roll.

Cairngorm.

THE summit gained !   And one, with down-bent eyes,
In rain-washed hollows, white with gravel bare,
Full keenly looks, now here his glance, now there,
And fruitless looks, till, lo ! a sudden prize
Gleams in the net of patience, and he cries
Loud of his luck.   Eager to him repair
A wide-eyed group, his boyish glee to share
As in spread palm brown prism of pebble lies !
But I, withdrawn, was gazing o'er the scene—
North, where the sea scarce differs from the cloud ;
East, where Ben A'an stares back with solemn mien ;
Or south-west, where the Badenoch clan-hills crowd.
My Cairngorm goodlier than his, I ween :
But what I found I could not tell aloud.

On Herrera.

"IF you are for the Castle, take the way
That goes by the shore." So said the kindly lass
Whose smiles a hostess made her, as our glass
Of milk she brought. She had not heard us say
Aught of the craggy keep in the far bay.
We had not known of the ruins. But to pass
Gold hours poured out uncounted, 'mid the grass
And heather, was our plan, the livelong day;
Feel the free wind, hear the sea-mew's wild cry,
Or cluck of the brown burn within the brake.
Yet, "If you are for the Castle," did me make
Thoughtful.—To the old walls then do all hie?
Yes! human story ever the heart must take;
Sacred the places where men live and die.

F

Ben Cruachan.

TAYNUILT! Forth stepping in the morning air,
Pleasant with scent of thyme, bog-myrtle, heath,
The eager Awe's soft freshness, Etive's breath,
We ask if there is track o'er shoulder bare
Where ascent is easy; and are answered—"There,"
With wave of the hand, "is the mountain!" hood
Of grey-white mist revealing it where it stood.
Could tell no more; 'twas left to us to dare
The summit as we might, finding our way.
Lesson of life! There, cloud-wrapt, is its peak;
Of trodden path for me no guide may speak.
Upwards, o'er moss and stone, through mists, must strain
Each traveller for himself, in his short day,
If haply he the hidden height may gain.

At Oban.

PRAY, can you tell which is the Pulpit Hill?

I did not know, and but expressed regret.

Then to myself soon, Strange so to forget!

The pastor-spirit might have taught thee skill

Wisely to speak; but give fit answer still

To other ears than those of querist met;

Blessing her for a mind to thinking set,

So that with pouring fancies it 'gan fill.

The Pulpit Hill! For answer look around!

'Tis each you see, blue-canopied with sky—

Ben Cruachan, from which law-thunders sound;

Ben More, in whose white sun-glints you espy

Feet of peace-preaching angels touch the ground:

From all the heights God's word comes variously!

At Brixham, Torbay.*

'TIS hewn, and shaped, and polished, now, that stone
Which William's foot first pressed two hundred years
Ago; it is railed round; and it uprears
Upon its obelisk point, on quay blast-blown,
A lamp, oft hailed as it has helpful shone,
By fishers straining towards the uncertain piers,
Their hope salt-dashed by breaking waves of fears—
To this the rude rock of old days has grown.
It is the Constitution of our land!
Rough did the wise Prince find it; now 'tis smooth—
Knowing since his of many a patriot hand
The fashioning touch—and guarded from unruth,
Here on the sea marge it doth strongly stand,
Lifting white light of liberty and truth!

* The Prince of Orange landed here, 1688.

On Enquiring the Way at an Old Forge, Devon.

THANKS, brother Vulcan, for the happy word :—

" This road to Totnes goes, good seven miles ;

And that," his grimed face flickering with smiles,

" Leads to the lanes, and," laughing as 'twere absurd,

" Oh, everywhere !" Thanks for the phrase I've heard.

Right brilliant sparks your hammer strikes oftwhiles,

And this is one ; its gleam my way beguiles ;

A pleasant debt to you I have incurred.

" Oh, everywhere !" 'Tis true of many a road :

It sets us thinking as free-souled we walk :

We pass to various scenes, at home, abroad ;

With friend half over the round world we talk

As o'er that fence ; or enter his abode

On prairie where red men were wont to stalk.

A Remote Waterfall.

Ten miles I walked, and five linked to the ten,

Then left the highway, entering a wood :

By wand'ring path long I my way pursued

'Mong heather and strewn rocks, the foxglove's den,

Till clear I was at last of the close glen—

When lo ! before me, as I sudden stood,

Over high cliff white-arching, a great flood

Poured thunderous, far from the world's ken.

Smit by sun's ray or star's, 'mid winter snow

Or June leaves, it is there ; and who would know

Its majesty, leaving the crowd behind,

Must journeying visit it.   Such is the mind

Of Greatness always : in its place it bides,

And would'st thou see it, go where it resides !

At the Castle of the Wartburg.*

'Tis the Grand Duke of Saxé Weimar's. So

The Guide Book tells me, with much sand-drift lore

'Bout lords and ladies great in days of yore;

And as my gaze wings o'er the landscape, lo!

Graved in the grass of yon hill side doth show—

Sight which my shaméd vision paineth sore—

A Crown, with letters after and before

Of the Duke's name. Him owner let all know!

But in my ear, "We're Luther's, Luther's!" cried

All things around. 'Before his loftier claim

Sinks title of earth's lordship from its pride;

Each hill displays unwrit the Reformer's name;

Than his I see no kingly crown beside:

He holds the land by right divine of fame!

* Where Luther was confined.

𝔚ait!

[A phenomenon of rare beauty, noticed in the papers at the time, was observed in some parts of Scotland at sunrise, 11th December, 1884.]

I.

BEAT with black wing against the pane the night,

Gusty and wild, and ever the weeping rain

Would wake me from my troubled sleep again;

And when the morning entered with dim light,

I heard the wet soak at the window sill.

"Another day of gloom, a drearier still!"

Such my complaining thought: "no more are bright

And glad-eyed dawns to greet us from the hill?"

Shaded in spirit, down to the morning meal

I took me, and by chance looked eastward out.

Scarce, as I gazed, repressed I sudden shout:

Lo! the clouds parting bands and peaks reveal

Of mother-of-pearl! God's glory strewn about!

Such a surprise of bliss who wake in heaven must feel.

II.

MANY the years were I had known the skies,

Marking them in their glory and their gloom;

Seeing the sun sink in his nightly tomb,

And in each morning's resurrection rise,

Smiling around with sleep-refreshéd eyes;

Yet never had such splendours been revealed.

And, O my God, what glories still concealed

Bide—as in boughs now bare the summer's bloom—

The appointed moment, and the mind's fine mood

In which the dreams from heaven are understood!

For Thy salvation teach my soul to wait;

Although it tarry, it will surely come,

What time my foot has told the meted sum

Of pilgrim steps that bring to the celestial gate.

At Chalfont St. Giles,* Buckinghamshire.

AND Milton walked these fields! Friend Ellwood's arm

Pressing, he paced full slow, amid the sounds

Of rural life; and, o'er the inwalling bounds

Of blindness borne, his spirit knew the charm

Of all the fair and summer-tinted world—

Saw the grey smoke at eve that thinly curled

'Bout the brown forehead of the ancient farm;

Saw on the plum-tree's staff the bloom unfurled.

He walks to-day! Reverend, his form appear

By pond or stile I mark. There on Church wall

His shadow moves. Christ, in yet nobler thrall

My homage hold! From this, that THOU art here,

Be consecration! This my joy in all—

Milton's high Lord and mine divinely near!

* Milton resided here for a time, in a house taken for him
by Ellwood, the Quaker.

To a Comet.

"CAUSED to fly swiftly," shining in white light,

On strenuous wing from the far court of heaven

Sped Gabriel. And, when the solemn even

Brought to the earth th' hour of oblation rite,

Softly he touched the prophet, tranced in prayer,

And, looking up, a glory Daniel saw,

His spirit trembling with a blissful awe;

While a still voice spake to his thrallèd ear :—

"To give thee skill, I've come, O man belov'd,

And teach thee understanding !" Even so,

Pale heavenly messenger, here from afar,

Hast thou this night me gently touched, and moved

My conscious soul with a new skill to know

How great the wonders of God's works and good-
    ness are !

On Enchinnan Bridge.

"The kingdom of God is within you."

HUNGRY for beauty, aching o'er for rest,
I left the dinsome town, and took my way
To where, methought, 'mong the far mountains lay
Buried the treasures. Eager in my quest
Up Enterkin's lone pass with seeking eye
I clomb; and, the wide summit reached, reclined,
Breast and hot brow bared to the bathing wind.
I saw th' empurpled hills, and the deep sky;
But not the beauty saw, or the rest found.
"They lie," then said I, "in the enchanted land
Where Yarrow flows"; and soon I gazing stand
On its sung banks, yet look in vain around.
Now, simple scene, in thee at my own door,
While seeking not, I find of peace full store!

At Hurstmonceux Castle.

THY very name's a charm! Ye red-white towers,

Loop-holed and ivy-hung, thou oriel fair,

Ye roofless walls, wing-swept by the free air,

Which carries scent of box and autumn flowers

From the old gardens, with their walks and bowers,

And memories too of Fiennes, Dacre, Hare—

Ye bear my spirit to a grander age!

Knights, dames, priests, servitors, rare figures old,

I seem to see wrought rich in cloth of gold,

Or shining on illuminated page.

Would that we lived once more in such great times,

Lulled into faith again by soft church chimes!

Thus dreamed I; then awoke to wiser mood—

Nay, Feudalism, 'tis in ruins thou art good!

Primrose Day : A Protest.

> "The nightingales,
> Their anthems of no church, how sweet they are!"
> —TENNYSON.

STILL from the very grave-mound will they take,

And for a challenge wear, the innocent flower

Large Heaven has given us as a common dower;

Teaching the lips of sweet-breathed Spring to break

God's truce in Nature, rather than whisper peace

Amid the strifes of Party, that increase?

With sunbeams and the showers, which have no creed,

Save God o'er all and pity for all need,

Leave the meek clusters ! For young children's hands,

From cottage or from castle, leave them ! Let the sick

At their cool touch feel on their beds release

From fever-fire that makes the blood boil quick !

Twist not God's blossoms in sectarian bands ;

Let them spell Love, gold-lettered, o'er the lands !

At Runnymede.

A PLAIN green field : yet what on thee has grown !—

Strong Liberty ! here planted by mailed hand

Of patriot peers, when John our English land

Scornful would hold for pleasaunce of his own.

Ringed with seven hundred years, to wide-girthed tree

The slip has waxed, bearing the useful fruit

Of laws ; and, seeding, on Thames' waters free

Has shed quick germs, which wave-born have ta'en root

On shores uprisen in the lonely sea

For homes of Greater England yet to be.

A plain green field : but to the freeman's eye,

Seen from afar amid time's haze of gold

To hero-guise transformed thy barons bold,

Thou seem'st a shining valley of the sky !

On a Former Business Coat of Arms.

(MACMILLAN AND CO.)

THREE acorns : triple seed of purpose strong.

Higher, on the right hand, a bee : for not

By growth alone, if industry day long

Be wanting, may achievement be outwrought.

And to life's task be music, as bee's song,

Be lightsomeness and charm of beauty brought,

In their fit place : for such the pleasant thought

Which on the left that butterfly has hung.

Now lo ! above have fruited in three stars

The acorns : telling of accomplished aims.

And 'tis within a cross's holy bars

All lie, while it a mystic sphere enframes :

Aim, effort, end, in that sign of high wars,

Itself within the circle which The Perfect names !

At Girban.

A BREEZY day 'mid yellow Autumn fields !
Dash of bunched foliage, twitter of small leaves,
Rustle of ears, crest of yon billowy sheaves;
Waft of keen fragrance the strewn sea-weed yields ;
A sudden stillness where this thick wall shields,
Then gathered murmuring from far and near,
As when a shell's smooth lip kisses the ear.
Noise of a nearing train among the hills,
Hoarse as the sea, then faint like far-off rills,
Then loud again—I start with foolish fear !
A dog barks distant. Now a robin sings,
Better food bearing than the ravens brought.
I hear and see and feel, and have no thought :
Soul-satisfied with sense of simple things.

The Handel Festival, 1885.

I.

BICENTENARY of his birth ! 'Tis well

To mark this advent of a life : of death

We think not, for the forceful breath

Of immortality blows in these sounds ;

That mighty utterance knows no temporal bounds ;

For ever on the far-drawn billows swell,

And pour themselves in grand melodious tide,

While children of new generations clap

Rejoicing hands, as the great waves in ride,

And breaking thunderous the shook shore wrap.

Nor only in his song doth he abide :

To soul creative, unto God allied

By power to praise Him, never could it hap

That pen should write, ON SUCH A DAY HE DIED !

II.

FIVE thousand instruments and voices, one !

White hands show as they move, shuttling the bows

Which music weave; flutes pipe; strong trumpet
blows;

Choir-cloud on the right hand, now sudden cleft,

Peals mellow thunders, echoed from the left—

As if to sister brother angels spoke,

And sisters answered, from each side God's throne.

By no harsh dissonant note's the harmony broke.

Oh, when, great Christ, conductor of earth's choir,

Shall men obey Thee, keeping Thy perfect time,

Each bearing his part with each in fitting chime,

Each voice, each instrument, now low, now higher,

True to the silent beat of Thy desire !

Then Heaven will bend to hear earth's strains
sublime.

At the Watersmeet, Lynmouth.

I.

DOWN wood-hung path, with honeysuckle sweet,
Through gloom of ferns lighted with fox-glove's glow,
We wend our way, silent with thought and slow,
Nearing the music of the Watersmeet.
And resting now, stretched upon mossy seat,
We watch the brown-cheeked water trembling go,
With foam-white feet, to trysting place below;
While, round yon corner, amorous and fleet,
Comes her bold lover.   Straight in soft embrace
The twain are locked; then hand in hand they run,
Young gladness glancing from each dimpled face,
Or, at monition of the looking sun,
Reflective grown, steal on with sober pace :
Their moods the same, their actions ever one.

II.

And what draws feet of pilgrims to this spot?

'Tis not the fairest nook of all the scene.

Here baldest cliffs and whitest falls are not,

Or massiest rocks velvet with freshest green ;

Elsewhere the trees tip higher the blue serene.

The charm's not that of scenery, but of thought,

The thread of sentiment with all inwrought,

The something which these meeting waters mean.

The human in them moves us, that which tells

Of our lives' myst'ries—how they meet and twine,

And flow together, with their lulls and swells,

Their breaks and eddies, in the shade or shine,

Gloomy 'neath cliff, or bright with sunny bells ;

My sorrow yours, your gladness also mine.

On an Earnest Face at a Gospel Meeting.

IT was not beautiful that grave young face
Fixed on God's messenger, whose pleading call,
Like a wave-heaving wind, moved spirits all.
There, as I looked, no soft-swept lines of grace,
Filled in with peachy bloom, the eye could trace.
No rose her cheek, no faint-flushed pearly shell
Her little ear, with convoluted swell.
Yet did that countenance my soul enthrall.
'Twas awe-transfigured, as in Holiest Place
The high priest's !　Clear from earth's bestaining clay
Was the rapt spirit, gazing far away !
A seraph's look I saw, through sense-veil riven,
Or that as of a dear dead child in heaven.
Great human face, that lights in God's eye-ray !

In Westminster Abbey.

March, 1885.

"AGE of machines, digging and crushing gold,

Shaping and stamping it, pouring the grain

Of specie out, which gleams like sun-smit rain---

Hard iron age! unlike the times of old

When worth lived simple in plain Nature's eye,

Finding its gold in crocus or eve's sky—

Thy god is mammon, millionaires thy saints,

Thy heaven success, confession of sin complaints

Of miscarrying ventures!" Such my bitter moan,

Entering Westminster for one breath of th' air

Of other days;—when the word LIVINGSTONE

Looks up at me, cut in that blue slab there;

And as to Poet's Corner my eye turns,

I read rebuke again in new-carved bust of BURNS!

" 𝕭𝖑𝖎𝖓𝖉."

Picture of an Old Lion, by A. T. Nettleship,
Grosvenor Gallery, 1883.

BLUE haze of blindness in the old mournful eyes

That know not of the cliff one paw o'erlaps.

Beneath gapes death; another step he lies

Stiffened below, while over him foul flaps

The vulture's wing. And, see, already slink

Cowardly about him, to the invisible brink

Herding him on, a vile hyena pack,

Red-mouthed and soft of foot. So to me shows

Old Milton, sightless, "fallen on evil days

And evil tongues," destroyers at his back.

Turn but the kingly head round on such foes,

The dull and lightless orbs would seem to blaze;

The dastard crew obscene, scattered and cowed,

Knowing the lightning sheathed within the cloud.

Lux e Tenebris.

HAVE faith, my soul, thy clouding care will pass !

This morn the mist lay thick o'er all the scene,

Scarce visible the tallest tree-top green :

No rift of pleasant blue, no glint of grass,

The air opaque as breath-bedimmèd glass.

But ere the dull sands of the day had run,

Forth looked in radiance the late-sleeping sun :

The gloom was gone as it had never been ;

And I who sat dejected in the grey,

Gazing at even from a gleam-tipped height,

Saw, o'er the landscape lessening far away,

The open west a sea of liquid light,

With one tree 'gainst it black in bough and spray,

And one winged cloud, a fly in the amber bright !

Iona.

As one who on the road, among the stones,

Should chance upon a pebble richly graved,

Storied with priestly forms and saintly cross,—

So come we on Iona 'mid the isles.

Its emerald surface history's burin owns ;

Tracing to thought how mild Columba braved

Wild waves and wilder men, at th' enriching loss

Of all that wins a witless world's smiles.

Here piety prevailed from granite bare

Beauty to create, firm-knit with majesty,

Then breathed into the frame a soul of prayer.

Such mystic meanings grow beneath mine eye.

The gem I take, upon my breast to wear :

One travel-memory more, rest sacred there !

Staffa.

IONA holy, this but common ground!

Because no temple made with hands is here,

Or carven crosses sacred forms uprear,

No consecrated tombs lie solemn round?

This, too, is temple, pillared more profound:

By God's hand raised each shapely shaft severe;

The sea-mew's scream is worship in His ear;

Well pleased He hears the sweeping billows sound.

Within the cave, Elijah's soul is mine,

Or Moses', when " Thy glory show!" he prayed.

I stand thought-wrapt, most blissfully afraid.

Man is not, all is God; an awful shrine

These columned stones and arching roof have made.

To-day I know the earth to be divine.

Stonehenge and Salisbury Cathedral.

Up rose from columned Stonehenge on quick wing

A bird, nor rested from far flight until

On floriated chancel-window's sill

Of Sarum's minster it sank fluttering.

Of my mind's flying with it do I sing.

A spiritual flight: not over hill,

Or field, or road, but years of good and ill,

And the strange good that God from ill doth bring.

Stonehenge, Salisbury—be they symbols styled!

Of blood as vainly as unwilling spilt,

One speaks; of Christ self-given for a world's guilt,

The other. Vi'lence that; this manners mild.

Stonehenge! grim blocks as for a prison piled;

Salisbury! fair Father's house of smooth stones built.

Glasgow Exhibition, 1888.

Yes, yes, I'll come ; be sure your mile-spread tent

On the May-mead will draw my loyal feet.

Inventions, pictures, products rare that meet

From many lands, in friendly vieing sent,

On the long floors artistically blent,

Rich Royal presents, quaint Old Glasgow's street—

All my pleased eye will welcomefully greet,

My spirit glad with wine of wonderment.

Yet would I rather steal some common day

Back 'mid old scenes, lonely to move about,

Looking for what the years have borne away :

See Campsie's fell, that o'er the smoke looks out,

Kelvin, or Clyde, where I was wont to stray,

Or the plain street that heard my boyhood's shout.

A Saint.

ON A PICTURE OF A PEASANT WOMAN BY J. F. MILLET.

"SALUTE the beloved Persis," said St. Paul

To the Church at Rome; and thee, saint of to-day

We greet, thus meeting on life's common way.

No shining task is thine, observed of all:

Thou toilest screened within thy garden small.

Thy plot of ground tended with faithful care,

Thy hearthstone white, thy children taught their

    prayer—

Happier thy husband than the squire in hall.

Thy cap's a nimbus round thy honest head;

Eye upon work is as in worship bent;

Prayer thy grave face, thine arms in toil outspread;

That gathered fruit into the basket shed

An offering poured to God doth represent.

"Much in the Lord thou, too, hast laboured!"

Age and Youth.

OLD tower that totters on the wave-worn rock;

Old trees that pause for breath half up the hill;

Old stones with moss white-bearded; bowed old mill;

Old church with lichened walls and quaint-faced clock;

Old gravestones in old churchyard, a grey flock;

Old sexton whose thinned spade old mould doth fill—

All things are old, look wheresoe'er I will:

The world dies palsied from full many a shock.

Who could dream of the future now, or think

Of travelling abroad, of winning fame

Or wealth, or being wed? Done world, adieu!

So spoke I with fool's tongue; for the light chink

Of a boy's laugh from near me silvery came,

And in his young eye's ray beheld I all things new.

At Brantwood, Coniston.

THE RESIDENCE OF JOHN RUSKIN.

Here at calm eve, sunk in thy rustic chair,

Through yellowed leaves lookst thou with age-mild eye.

Over the lake doubtful thou dost espy

Amid the foliage, buildings here and there,

'Minished and blended by the gracious air.

Where house of rich man or of poor doth lie,

Or chapel or church, thou canst not sure descry :

Only of man and God art thou aware.

Thou blessest both.   Railway which scars the hill,

Steam-launch on mere, with smoke and whistle shrill,

Mar not the "glory" of the mount and cloud,

And arch of blue, and one star in the west.

All seen in that, pass with thy grey head bowed,

"Lamp of the Infinite" lighting thee, to rest !

All Things are of Thee.

" 'Tis only noble to be good !"   Well spake

The poet preaching; and I preacher may

Dare to be poet and responsive say :

'Tis good too to be noble !   Do not make

High truth eclipse the low : warm Mars doth take

The eye with his redness, while the diamond ray

Of Venus compensates the loss of day :

From various strings God's fingers music wake.

The sun, which has no virtue nor adores ;

The unconscious iceberg flashing in far sea ;

Niagara, which no libation pours ;

A statue, standing in mere majesty ;

A mighty intellect, that but explores ;—

Are they not good in that they noble be ?

H

The Poet's Teachers.

"WE learn in suffering what we teach in song."
In gladness too : joy speaks to me to-day,
Its white rose out upon life's brier-spray.
Brisk hops the bird that blossomed bough along,
And yonder, on the daisied grass, a throng
Of happy children mingle at their play :
Kaleidoscopic forms that change alway.
I feel what 'tis rejoicing to be strong !
Man, know thyself when thou art glad of heart,
'Tis only then thou knowest worthily;
In likeness of His bliss God fashioned thee ;
Sorrow, like sin, is of an alien part,
Nor will our life be a fit melody
Till joy has taught us the true singer's art.

MISCELLANEOUS POEMS.

A Smile.

LIKE the sky with sunbeam,

Like a room with fire-gleam,

How a face is lit up with a smile !

I saw it to-day,

As I toiled on my way,

And it shortened the road a good mile.

How the eye kindles bright,

And the teeth sparkle white—

Ivory keys o'er which joy's fingers run—

How the dimpled cheeks shine

With a radiance benign !

My heart feels the touch of their sun.

Mighty magic of MIND,

By the flesh unconfined,

Writing quick with unseen spirit hand !

What mysteries lurk,

What deep-hid powers work,

Then flash in the face at thy wand !

Just one little word said—

It is life from the dead ;

How the features, so sombre and still,

Become suddenly bright

With gold ripples of light,

Raised by the wind-touch of thy will !

Give me, dear Christ, love's heart,

As the true better part,

Blesséd storage of sunshine within !

That each new day I live

I some gladness may give,

And smile away some cloud of sin.

Messengers.

IT lighted on me as I lay,
  Stretched 'neath a bank's eaves from the rain ;
And ere it had fluttered away,
  It stirred a sweet thought in my brain.

Close shut were the leaves of its wings ;
  I saw them of gloomy black-brown,
Faint figured with crosses and rings,
  And feathered with finest of down.

Funereal-plumed butterfly !
  Your lighting so soft made me start ;
Away ! was my unuttered cry,
  As I felt sudden throbbing of heart.

The dusky-hued bud-wings unfold—

What blossom bursts forth on the sight!

Lustrous " eyes " of bright purple and gold,

With stainings of red, brown, and white.

Long resting, the fair creature stays,

And as all its splendour I see,

God sent you, my happy heart says,

On errand of teaching to me :

How trouble, in raiment so sad,

Is only a joy with shut wings :

They open ; and straightway we're glad

With vision of glorious things !

The east had been cavernous gloom,

But now 'tis with twin rainbows spanned ;

Like the angels that guarded Christ's tomb,

Wing close to tinged wing as they stand.

Oh, glory-plumed rainbows on high !

Oh, butterfly low on my knee !—

Bit of colour dropt out of the sky—

Ye bring the same lesson to me :

That after the dark comes the light,

And the great God is beauty and love :

You tell it me, butterfly bright,

And ye, seraph rainbows above !

In the mouths of the witnesses two,

Soft speaking to me in my need,

The word is establishéd true,

That gloom is of glory the seed.

The bows in the heaven paled away,

The butterfly rose on the wind :

The messengers here could not stay,

But they left their message behind.

Simple Happiness.

A BROWN-ROOFED cot was in sight,
  With pigeons round it straying,
And a man working in a field,
  And little children playing.

And the air was sweet and cool,
  The autumn sun was shining,
Bright was the creeper on the wall—
  Red, gold, and green combining.

Nothing of the world's was mine,
  But I felt rich in pleasure,
And I blessed my God in my heart,
  Who had given me such treasure.

I found it hid in the field,

What time I was not seeking :

" Ask *not*, and ye shall receive "—

That also is Christ speaking.

In a Suburban Street.

A CARTFUL of garden cuttings
  Laid by the side of the road,
And three pretty children picking
  Sprigs from the tempting load.

One of them looked at me smiling,
  As if she had known me well;
But 'twas only the simple pleasure
  Her innocent eyes must tell.

I threw back a smile; and passing
  Happy along the street,
A few steps farther onwards
  A lady I chanced to meet.

My eye on hers carelessly lighting,

Demurely she fixed her face;

And I sighed, Alas, that experience

Should make us distrust our race !

A Winter Morning.

New snow white on old thatch,
  Berries red on grey tree,
Gleam of smooth prick-edged leaves—
  A lesson writ for me.

God with His frost makes fair
  The roof smoky and torn ;
Bright berries speak Him kind,
  Though the leaves point their thorn.

I feel the north wind keen ;
  But it blows out of blue,
And as I walk, the blood
  Dances my glad veins through.

All things come to us mixed,

What is there simply good?

When was a blessing sent

As the receiver would?

Humbly I take the boon

I do not understand,

Placed in the shadow cast

By the great giving Hand.

A Vanished Scene on the Clyde.

OFT have I looked for them since,
　Those solemn dark hills and high,
With, against them, the storm-birds white,
　As seen by my childhood's eye.

Time after time have I sailed
　Down the dear stream to the sea ;
The very same stream where the hills
　And the birds were seen by me.

But never the dark high hills,
　Nor the white birds borne like foam,
Would again to the longing eye,
　Out from the emptiness come.

I

How had the black mountains sunk?
　Where was their wild grandeur gone?
Why were there no great white birds
　Now sailing solemnly on?

Ah me! is it childhood's sight,
　Not mountain or bird, that's fled?
The morning mist, making all large,
　Is't that from the landscape's sped?

In mystic memory alone
　Can the dark high hills be seen?
And the great white birds borne like foam,
　Had these but in youth's eye been?

Fret not! your boy's eye to-day
　Sees the shut glories unfold;
'Tis his turn on the Father's knee
　To have the old stories told.

A New Early Summer.

Just as in by-gone years !
  The leaf comes out on the tree,
The early swallow appears,
  The cowslips sprinkle the lea.

Just as in by-gone years!
  The lark is loud in the sky,
Sounds as long since in the ears
  The hum of the passing fly.

Just as in by-gone years !
  Warm feels the touch of the sun,
Darkens the heaven or clears,
  As it for ever hath done.

All as in by-gone years !

Yet nothing's the same to me—

Voices the ear no more hears,

Faces the eye cannot see.

Simple Wisdom.

I WILL not now question at all,
   But take the world just as it is ;
Whatever events may befall,
   I will look up and say they are His.

My heart I will ope to the sun,
   To the night chills I'll fold up its leaves ;
When the rain falls its pelt I will shun,
   Smiling out 'neath some sheltering eaves.

When it freezes I'll draw near the fire,
   At the darkening I'll light up my room,
When the blaze sinks I'll pile the coals higher,
   With brightness I'll battle the gloom.

I will suit myself all that I can

  To the world the Wise Ruler has made ;

Remembering the law of His plan—

  For each thing its price must be paid.

No longer I'll say, Why is this ?

  But This is, and I've been put here.

That simple obedience is bliss,

  The child knows, the man learns full dear

The Ignorant Peasant.

'Twas not three miles off, but she could not tell
  The way to the village of Lyne;
It lay out of sight, for the ground took a swell
  And hid the small hamlet of Lyne.

'Twas near three miles off, and how could she know
  So distant a place as was Lyne?
It had nought to do with her matters, I trow :
  No kinsfolk of hers lived in Lyne.

As for her, here in Thorpe, hard by yon tree,
  She dwelt, and knew nothing of Lyne;
She might ask her man, Will, but didn't think he
  Had ever heerd mention o' Lyne.

She went to church, yes, and knew Christ and God :

　But nothing could tell me of Lyne ;

And she loved little Will, long under the sod :

　But no, she knew nothing of Lyne.

She'd not say me false, good soul, for her life,

　And could not direct me to Lyne :

A God-fearing woman, kind mother and wife,

　And yet to know nothing of Lyne !

Well, let us thank God she at least knew Heaven,

　Though ignorant so as to Lyne,

And loved her two Wills : 'tis not to all given

　To be learned and know about Lyne.

"This Great Sight."

Far down in the depths of the forest,
  Aside in loneliest spot
'Mid oaks old, of patriarchs hoarest,
  By woodcutter death long forgot,

There flashed forth ablaze all with glory,
  Its lit leaves of reddest gold,
A beech like the bush in the story
  Beheld by the prophet of old.

Why here in this solitude hidden,
  Where scarce there's a passer-by?
Why, catching the greenwood, thus redden
  The flames to no noticing eye?

'Tis enough if one awe-stricken Moses

God's glory there burning see :

To the prophet the desert discloses

The vision he tells you and me !

Where is Thy God?

THERE were foxgloves bright by the road,
  And there crossed it a gold-mailed fly,
Ferns shook from the lichened grey wall:
  I felt that the dear God was nigh.

Oh! Maker of simple fair things—
  Fly, foxglove, moss, ivy, and fern—
Thy love in these lovely I know,
  Thee great in these little I learn!

Walking on, I came to a bird:
  Blood-stained were its feathers of grey;
A touch of a blind passing wheel
  Had crushed out its life where it lay.

Ah, now not so clear saw I God :

A mist had come up o'er mine eyes :

It rose as I looked at the bird

   Flat there on the roadway that lies.

And I lose Him more as the tombs

   Of the hamlet's churchyard I reach—

'Tis there on that slope by the sea :

   The waves requiem chant on the beach.

Hid by the close-standing gravestones

   —One tells of an infant so small,

And one of a dear husband drowned—

   He scarce can be seen now at all.

Alas ! I've lost sight of Thee, God,

   Whom this morn, low bent on my knees,

I "Father" in prayer had called,

   Saying, "Do Thou the things that Thee please!"

Seen bright 'mid the harebells and ferns,

  Thy face darkened out by the way

To this place of cold tomb-cast shade

  From the spot where the bruised bird lay.

It is orphaned eyes that I lift,

  When lo ! on a pillar, white-cut

With chisel unfalt'ring, there gleam

  Words of One who had "Sparéd not

"His Own Son, but for us men all

  Delivered Him up," in sweet grace ;

And as I gazed, soul-held, my God,

  Again from the gloom came Thy face.

I knew it at first not so well

  As I thought I had done before,

When seen where the foxgloves and ferns

  Light-hearted I bent myself o'er.

There was a shade dark in thine eyes;
Thou too, Father, seemedst to grieve:
And in Thy love which I less knew
The more my awed heart did believe.

So, bramble with harebell and fern
In chaplet of *faith* I now twine;
I shadow the foxglove with yew,
For the dark and the bright are Thine.

On this gravestone I hang the wreath,
Here by the black sun-glinted sea,
Near the road where the wheel-crushed bird
And gay foxgloves were seen by me.

I praise Thee, my God, found and lost,
And found to be lost not again:
Earth's ills can no more make me doubt—
Of Thy love I've seen the blood-stain.

Lo! the darkness lifts from the grave:
Drowned sailor and little one dead,
Christ low, in His sympathy sweet,
Beside yours laid down His pierced head.

As if with His arm round you each,
You sleep, and together you'll rise,
His known face the first thing you see,
Heaven's dawn in the look of His eyes!

On an Old Portrait.

FULL eye, rose-leaf lip, living warm flesh and blood,'
And a hundred and ten years ago :
How strange 'tis to gaze and to think of thee thus,
And to know thee so long lying low !

In Seventeen Eighty the summer sun shone,
There were flowers in the grass as to-day,
And heart throbbed to heart as hands touched at
the stile,
In that far-a-way fair month of May.

They were living and young then, the long long dead,
Their strong forms and bright faces I see ;

Old age and the grave? oh, far off! and they
    laughed,
And false echo laughed back to their glee.

My great-grandsire's young head I see by yon chair,
    As he bends to the spinnet, where sits
A sunny-haired maiden, across whose blue eyes
    Just a gleam of sweet consciousness flits.

And is there not left now a little dark dust,
.   From a frame that had mouldered slow,
With lip of rose-leaf fold, and eye that looked love,
    All a hundred and ten years ago?

Ah! is *Carpe diem* the one wisest word
    Which the tongue of poor mortal may speak?
To canvas age-blackened and scarred must we turn
    The loved forms of the long-lost to seek?

K

Nay, 'tis not the dead that I look upon here,

There's a prophet's word writ on the page :

As the face in the picture is young yet to-day,

So the spirit-face knoweth not age !

To Ailsa Rock.

Lone, where blue sea of sky, blue sky of sea

Meet, Ailsa, thou art to me as a star

By which I my soul's bearings take afar,

Measuring its mystic place in things from thee.

Sunned or cloud-capt,—beauty, sublimity,

Thou showest; age's hoar, strength amid war

With billows passion-white, which back beat are;

Thy form, too, altar unto Deity!

From thine my life how little, weak, I learn—

A sun-gleam or a gloom upon thy brow.

Yet I'm the observer, the mere measure thou!

The fair, great, ancient, in thee, I discern!

Cloud on thee as oblation-smoke I know!

And while thou'rt fixed, my free soul on doth go!

PRINTED AT THE UNIVERSITY PRESS, BY
ROBERT MACLEHOSE, 153 WEST NILE STREET, GLASGOW